Them
and Us

Check out Bali's website
www.balirai.co.uk

Them
and Us

Bali Rai

Five Leaves Publications
www.fiveleaves.co.uk

Them and Us
Bali Rai

Published in 2016 by Five Leaves Publications
14a Long Row, Nottingham NG1 2DH
www.fiveleaves.co.uk
www.fiveleavesbookshop.co.uk

ISBN: 978-1910170380

Them and Us
was first published
by Barrington Stoke in 2009

Designed and typeset by
Four Sheets Design and Print

Printed in Great Britain

Contents

Chapter 1

Another New Start

My mum put the shopping bags down and took a long look round the room. We were standing in the kitchen of our new flat and it was really small. It was also very dirty.

"David — can you help me clean this place up?" she asked me.

I nodded as I ran my finger across the worktop. There was a thick layer of grease on it, which turned my fingertip black.

"This place is crap," I said.

"David," begged my mum. "You don't have to swear."

I shook my head.

"Yeah, I do," I told her. "We ain't supposed to be here, are we?"

My mum gave a shrug. She looked well tired. And I could see the worry lines on her face.

"It's not anyone's fault," she said.

"Yeah, it is!" I shouted. "It's that knob's fault!"

The knob was my dad. Not that I liked calling him that. So what if he was my dad? He was a tosser. Because of him we'd spent the last three years just moving from one crappy flat to another. We'd lived all over the city and I'd been to so many different schools that I couldn't even remember them all. I was always the new kid thanks to him. I *hated* him.

"Just pass me the bleach," said my mum. "I'd better get started. I've gotta go to work at three."

When I was younger my dad was in prison. He was doing time for manslaughter but I didn't know much about it. I knew that my mum was scared of him and I knew that he was trouble but not much else. But when I was ten, he came home. At first my mum seemed OK with it. It looked as if maybe he'd changed. He even took me to football and that. But after six months he was beating me and Mum up. He was always drunk and on drugs and his dodgy mates spent all their time at our flat. My best mate back then was an Asian lad called Binny and my dad hated him. He hates anyone that ain't white and English. He's even got these racist tattoos all over his arms and back.

The first time Binny came round to play after my dad moved back in, there was trouble.

Binny had been in the flat for two minutes when my dad slapped me round the head.

"What's this Paki bastard doin' in my house?" he shouted.

"He's come to play," I said. I was trying not to cry.

"Not in my house, he ain't!" yelled my dad. "Get rid of him."

Binny was always really shy and I could tell that he was scared. He told me that he was going but I got angry.

"Just stay," I said.

My dad went mental. He kicked me in the arse and then punched me so hard that my nose broke. Then he grabbed Binny by the neck, dragged him to the door and threw him out onto the landing.

"Get out!" he shouted. Then he slammed the door shut.

Things like that happened all the time. The day after I turned twelve, my mum took us away. We went to stay with my nan on the other side of town. We wanted to hide — but Dad found us. My nan called the police and they took him away, kicking and screaming. But we knew then we couldn't stay with her. My mum said Dad was too dangerous.

"He'll have a go at your nan," she told me. "I'm sorry, David, but we gotta move."

That was three years ago and Mum's been saying the same thing ever since. It don't matter where we go or what we do, the arsehole finds out. I guess we could have moved to another city but my mum is too proud to do that.

"I ain't leavin' my friends and family 'cos of him," she'll say. "He can do one!"

This new flat was horrible. It was dirty and it stank. We'd only spent one night in it and I didn't want to help clean it up. But my mum was knackered — totally worn out. I didn't want her to clean it on her own. She worked as a nurse and she had a shift to go to. So I grabbed some cloths and a bottle of bleach and gave her a hand.

We'd moved to St Pauls. It's part of the city that's full of the people my dad hates. After I'd finished cleaning, I went out for a walk and I didn't see another white person for ages. It was weird. Some of the locals gave me funny looks and as I was standing outside a newsagent, eating a Mars bar, these two Asian lads rode by on mountain bikes. One of them threw an empty can at me.

"Oi!" I shouted after them.

They stopped and turned around.

"You want summat, white boy?" one of them asked.

I looked him right in the eye but didn't say anything.

"You must have got lost," said the other one. "This is *our* area."

Then they rode off, laughing as they went.

When I got in I turned on the telly and got a packet of crisps from the kitchen. The flat was a lot cleaner but there was still a really bad smell. Mum had gone to work and she'd left me a note about my new school. I started the next morning but already I didn't want to go. I flicked channels for a bit before I fell asleep on the sofa.

I woke up in the middle of the night, sweating. I'd had a bad dream. That was nothing new. In this dream my dad had found us again and he was standing by my bed with a sharp knife in his hand. He was smiling at me and I was scared, like when I was ten. I pulled a cushion over my face to hide but he pulled it back, and then tried to stab me. That was when I woke up. I went into the kitchen to get some water and stood there, praying that he wouldn't find us again. And then I started to worry about my new school.

Chapter 2

White Boy

I saw the difference when I walked into school for the first time. Just like on the streets, most of the people there were Asian or Black. And most of them were interested in me too. As I sat in front of the school office some of the other pupils walked past, saying things and pointing. Not that it bothered me. I'd been the new kid loads of times and it was always like that. I was there about ten minutes when a male teacher came and said hello.

"Hi, David," he said to me and held out his hand for me to shake. "I'm Mr Lester. Welcome to Wayside."

I shook his hand and stood up, ready for him to take me to my class. But he didn't do that.

"The school is pretty big," he said. "I'll show you around and then I've got two students from your class coming to get you."

I nodded. Mr Lester was tall and he had

really wide shoulders. His hair was blond, the same shade as mine.

"It's a friendly school," added Mr Lester. "I think you'll like it here."

"Yeah," I replied, softly.

We went through some doors and down a long corridor with classrooms on both sides. Every now and then some of the pupils watched us pass. One or two of them turned round and knocked on the glass as we walked past. I ignored them.

Mr Lester was right about the school being big. Wayside was massive. There were four huge blocks, all four floors high. In the middle sat a lower block with offices and staff rooms. Then there were separate assembly and dinner halls and a sports hall which sat on its own across the field from the car park.

"It's easy to find your way round the school," Mr Lester told me. "Each of the blocks has a letter and every floor has a number. You just have to remember which subjects are taught where. For example, I'm teaching you English. That's always in Block A, top floor ..."

I nodded at him.

"That's going to be A4," I said.

"Exactly," he replied with a grin. "And then each room on each floor has a number ... mine is Room One. On your timetable it'll say English — A4-01 ..."

I told him I understood but I wasn't really listening. I'd seen two lads eyeing me from one of the classrooms and I was staring back at them. I'd been the new kid so many times, I knew some of the lads would try it on with me. They'd try and bully me to see what I did. If I backed down, they'd know I was weak and carry on. But if I stood up to them, then they'd leave me alone. At least, that's what I thought.

The two pupils who took me around were OK. One of them was a lad called Faizal and the other one a girl. She was called Priya and she was cute. The lad told me to call him Faz.

"That's what everyone calls me," he said.

"Well, some people call him arse too," Priya joked.

Faz told her to get lost and we walked into Block B. Two lads were standing by the doors as we walked in. They were staring at me.

"That *bwoi* is gonna stick out round here,"

said one of the lads. He was about as tall as me with a big nose and wispy bits of hair on his top lip and chin. He had a cap on his head too. The other lad grinned.

"Easy, white boy!" he said to me.

I nodded to him.

"I'm David," I said.

The two lads looked at each other and started to laugh. Then they started talking to each other in some Asian language. I looked at Faz, who gave a shrug.

"Come on," he said. "Let's go ..."

I waited until we'd gone up the stairs before I asked him what the lads had said. Faz looked at Priya.

"Dunno," Faz said. "I don't speak that language."

Priya told me to forget about it.

"They're fools anyway," she said.

Faz stayed with me all morning and at lunch-time he took me into the dinner hall. I stood in the queue and looked around at the other pupils. There were loads of Asian kids and some black ones too but I didn't see a single white pupil. I stuck out a mile.

"Are there any other white kids at this school?" I asked Faz.

He nodded. "There's a few. Most of them are from Poland and other places."

"Oh," I said.

"But it's OK," Faz added. "Most of the kids here are nice and that ..."

Just as he spoke, Priya turned up with two other girls.

"This is David," she told her friends.

I smiled and said hello and the two new girls smiled back.

"I'm Samira," said one of them. She was short and slim and she was wearing a blue headscarf.

"And I'm Sonia," said the other one. She was taller than Samira and had curly brown hair.

"We're your new friends!" added Priya.

I looked at Faz, who was grinning at me.

"Check you out!" he said. "Big hit with the ladies already!"

I felt myself blush.

"We hang out in the library," Samira told me. "The woman who runs it is really nice."

I nodded. I didn't really read books but only because I never got any. But the few books I'd read at school had been OK.

"Plus it's the warmest place in the school," Priya added.

"You could come with us after you've had lunch," Sonia said.

I gave a shrug.

"I need to check out the rest of the school," I told them. "Try and get to know it."

Faz nodded.

"Don't worry," he told the girls, "he'll still be here tomorrow."

"But we're your best friends!" said Sonia in a silly voice.

Faz shook his head.

"Don't worry," he told me, "you'll get used to them three. They're mental ..."

When we'd finished eating Faz took me outside. There were three astro-turf football pitches on one side of the school and a big playing field on the other. In the middle was a concrete playground which was big too. Most of the other pupils were just hanging around, but Faz took me to the astro-turf pitches where a game of football was going on.

"Do you play?" he asked me.

I nodded. Football was one of my most favourite things. I loved it. Sometimes it felt like I was only happy when I was kicking a ball around.

"Let's join in, then," he said. "These lads are OK — most of them are my friends."

As we walked into the game Faz told some of the lads who I was. They were OK with me. We joined the same side and started to play. Most of the players weren't very good but Faz was great. He was strong on the ball and the other players found it hard to tackle him. On my first touch, a short Asian lad tried to tackle me but I held him off. I turned and skipped past two more lads and then I was in on goal. I shifted the ball to my left foot and cracked a shot at goal. It flew in.

"Yes, white boy!" someone shouted, as Faz came over.

"That was a wicked goal!" he said.

I gave a shrug.

"Suppose," I answered.

We played on for fifteen more minutes and I

scored another goal. When it was time to go back into lessons, Faz walked with me.

"There's a school team," he told me. "You should come along to the practice."

"I might," I said.

"Nah ... for definite," he added. "You're good!"

I nodded.

"OK," I said. "Just let me know when."

Faz opened the door for me as we walked into A-block.

"Wednesday, after school," he said. "Mr Lester is the coach."

As we walked up the stairs, the two lads I'd seen that morning went past us. They kept away from Faz but one of them, the tall one, bumped into me.

"Watch it!" he spat at me.

I stopped and looked at him.

"You bumped me, blood," I said.

The lad smirked.

"I ain't no blood of yours, white boy. Best you just go back to white man land, innit."

Faz grabbed my arm. "Come on," he said.

"Yeah, yeah," said the tall lad. "Run, white boy, run!"

Faz turned to the lad, who was called Yusuf. "Leave him alone," he told him.

Yusuf looked at his mate and then back at Faz.

"Ease off, Faz," he said in a nasty way. "You don't wanna get into it over some pale-faced fool."

Faz shook his head.

"You're a twat," he told Yusuf.

Yusuf and his mate walked off, grinning.

"Don't worry about them," Faz told me. "They're all mouth."

I nodded but I didn't believe him. There was something in Yusuf's face that told me he hated me. And he didn't even know me.

I knew that Yusuf and his mates would be back. I'd been the new kid so many times and I knew that was just how things went.

Chapter 3
Yusuf

When Wednesday came I didn't make it to football practice. Not because I didn't want to go. Because Yusuf and his mates caught up with me before I got there.

The day started off well but after lunch we had R.E. with a young teacher called Mr Abbas. He was really chilled out for a teacher. I thought the lesson would be good but then one of Yusuf's mates began to get at me. This guy was called Tahir.

I'd moved to the school in November so by now Christmas was only a few weeks away. Mr Abbas began his lesson by telling us how close Christmas was. Right away Tahir got on one.

"It ain't nuttin' to do with us," he told the teacher.

"I'm sorry?" asked Mr Abbas.

"Christmas, innit?" said Tahir. "It's a white man ting and there ain't many of dem round here ..."

Mr Abbas put down the pen he was holding and stared at Tahir.

"I'm not talking about race, Tahir," Mr Abbas began. "I wanted to talk about religious festivals and what they mean."

"Don't care," answered Tahir, as Faz and Sonia both told him to shut up.

"You don't know nuttin'," Tahir said to Sonia.

She shook her head.

"You're a dick," she told him. "What do you know anyway?"

"Language, Sonia," warned Mr Abbas.

"But he is," said another girl. "He ain't right in the head."

This time Tahir shook his head.

"Let him tell us what he thinks," Mr Abbas went on. "Then maybe we can set up a good debate — that's what this is all about. We should all be able to say what we think."

"Christmas is a white man ting, you get me?" said Tahir. He made some of the other lads snigger.

"Not always," Sonia answered back. "I'm a Muslim and in my family we have Christmas. We give presents and cards and that."

"Well, you ain't very good Muslims then are you?" said Tahir.

"Better than you," Sonia told him.

As they were arguing, I kept looking down. I didn't want to get involved. But Tahir had other ideas.

"Only man in here who gives a toss 'bout Christmas is white boy over there," he said.

Mr Abbas looked over at me.

"What do you think about it, David?" he asked me.

The clever thing would have been to say nothing. But sometimes my temper gets the better of me and Tahir was getting to me.

"Christmas is British," I told him. "It's the main festival in this country."

"Very true," agreed Mr Abbas. "90 per cent of this country is white," he said to the class.

"Not round here they ain't," said Tahir.

"But that's just in this area, Tahir," Mr Abbas pointed out.

"Yeah," said Faz, joining in. "Just 'cos you ain't ever been anywhere else. The whole country don't look like round here, you fool."

Tahir gave a shrug.

"Couldn't care less," he went on. "I ain't no white boy and I ain't no Christian. We shouldn't even celebrate white people tings at this school … that's what my dad says."

This time I shook my head and Tahir saw me.

"Don't shake your head at me," he said. "You ain't in charge round here. This is our country round here."

Mr Abbas started to pack up his bag. I saw he wanted to finish the debate but I decided to wind Tahir up.

"No, it ain't," I told him. "You're just as British as me."

Tahir went red and stood up.

"I ain't no stinkin' white man!" he spat out. "I'm Pakistani and proud."

I started to laugh.

"Where were you born?" I asked him.

"Here," he had to say. "So what?"

"Well, that makes you British, doesn't it," I said. "You ain't even from Pakistan."

"Yes, I am!" he said. "Being born here don't mean nuttin' to me. I ain't British."

Faz snorted.

"Course you are," he told Tahir. "And so am I — British Pakistani ..."

"And everyone can celebrate Christmas," I added. "It's not even about being Christian — not any more."

Mr Abbas told us to stop talking but Tahir didn't listen.

"You people think you can tell us what to do," he said to me. "But not round here. This is our area and if you don't like it you can get lost."

I looked at Mr Abbas and then at Faz. Then I turned to Tahir. "If I said that to you or called you brown boy all the time, like you call me white boy, I'd get in real trouble!" I told him.

"Get stuffed, you dirty stinking white *bas* ..." Tahir began to shout.

"ENOUGH!" said Mr Abbas, stopping him. "COME WITH ME!"

And with that Mr Abbas marched Tahir out of the class. When they'd gone, Sonia turned to me.

"We ain't all like him," she told me.

"I know," I said. "Thanks."

She grinned at me.

"No problem," she said.

At the back of the room I saw two of Tahir's mates staring at us. One of them said something to the other and then they looked away.

★★★

After school was over I remembered about football practice. My kit was back at the flat so I ran home to get it. It was only five minutes from the school, across a main road and past some shops. But I didn't make it. Yusuf and his crew were outside Lahore Fried Chicken as I ran past.

"Get him!" shouted Yusuf.

I was in trouble. I ran as fast as I could. If I got to my block, I could buzz in and lock Yusuf's crew out. But someone tripped me up and I fell over outside the Pound Shop. I crashed into a load of mops and buckets that were on sale.

I rolled over and put my arms over my face as they started to kick me. There were six of them and one of them was Tahir. He kicked me the hardest. My legs were killing me and my face was cut and bloody. I reached out for something to attack them with and felt a mop handle. I grabbed it and lashed out. I caught one of them and then the kicking stopped.

I got to my feet and wiped the blood from my mouth.

"You're dead, white boy!" I heard Tahir say.

I didn't wait for them to start again. I smacked Tahir in the face with the mop handle and then I cracked it against Yusuf's legs. Both of them yelped and then they were on me again. This time I stayed on my feet but I lost the mop handle. I started to use my fists but it was no good. There were too many of them. And then someone punched me under the chin and I went down ...

Chapter 4
Forget About It

When I came round, I was sitting on the floor of the Pound Shop. An old Muslim man was looking down at me. He had one of those prayer caps on his head and his beard was white. He looked worried.

"Are you OK?" he said. His accent was really strong.

"Yeah," I croaked.

My head was banging and my chest felt like it had been stamped on by an elephant. I stood up slowly and held onto the counter, which was already done up for Christmas.

The old man was still looking at me. He gave me some tissues. "I had to drag you in," he said. "I couldn't lift you or get you into a chair."

I looked at the door, past a load of Christmas trees and other decorations.

"They've gone," said the man. He knew that I was looking for Yusuf and his crew.

"I'm OK," I told him.

The man shook his head.

"You want me to call your parents?" he asked.

I shook my head.

"My mum ain't home," I lied. I didn't want him to make a fuss. I was hurt but not that badly. I just wanted to get out of there.

"You should stay a bit," the old man told me. "My name is Mr Abbas."

It hurt my face but I smiled all the same.

"My teacher's called that," I told him.

Mr Abbas smiled back.

"That is my son," he said. "He is teacher ..."

I nodded. "That's funny," I said. "I just had him for a lesson."

The old man looked really proud.

"He is good boy," he said. "Let me get you a drink or something."

"I'm fine," I said to him. "I just want to go home."

"OK," he said. "But if you want me to call the police or tell them what I saw, I'm happy to do it."

I said thank you, that it was OK.

"I just want to go home," I told him.

Mr Abbas wouldn't let me go home on my own. He closed the shop so that he could walk with me. I let him. The last thing I wanted was to bump into Yusuf and his mates again. At least not until I felt better. Then I was going to get them — all of them.

I thanked Mr Abbas again when we got to my block of flats. He said to come and say hello any time and then he walked off. I walked slowly up four flights of stairs and let myself in. I started to go to the bathroom. I wanted to clean up before Mum saw me.

"That you, David?" she shouted.

"Yeah," I shouted back.

"Got your tea on," she added.

Was I going to have to tell her what had happened? There was no way I could hide the cuts and bruises from her. And I always told her everything, not like with my dad. I gave a sigh and walked into the kitchen.

"OH, MY GOD!" she said and she grabbed hold of me. "What happened?"

I gave a shrug.

"Nothing," I told her. "Just some lads ..."

"What lads?" she asked me. *David?*

I leant back on the worktop and folded my arms.

"Just some lads from school," I began. "They beat me up."

She grabbed some kitchen towel and held it under the cold tap. Then she started to clean up my face.

"Right," she told me. "I'm off work tomorrow. First thing, we're goin' up that school."

I shook my head.

"No, Mum," I said. "I'm not grassing anyone up. That'll just give me more grief. Forget about it."

She stopped cleaning my face and looked at me.

"Is it because you're new?" she asked. I nodded.

"Just that?" she added.

I shook my head.

"What else then?" she asked.

I let her clean me up some more before I

talked some more.

"There's no other white kids at the school," I said. "Some of them pick on me."

My mum made a face.

"They do what?" she said.

"Not everyone," I told her. "Most of the kids are great but there's this crew of lads who don't like me 'cos I'm white."

She stopped again and gave me a puzzled look.

"Are you telling me that they're being racist towards you?" she asked.

I nodded.

"Don't worry," I told her. "It'll stop soon. It's not like this is the first time I've had trouble at a new school."

I hadn't meant to make my mum feel bad but that's what I'd done. She looked away. "I know it's my fault," she began. "All this moving around. It can't be easy for you ..."

"No!" I said as loud as I could. "It's not your fault. It's that tosser ..."

She put her hand on my face.

"I'm sorry, David," she said again.

I shook my head.

"It's not your fault," I said again. "You're great."

Later on, just before my mum had to leave for work, she came into the living room. There was some stupid talk show on and I wasn't really watching it.

"Talk to your teachers," she told me.

"I dunno," I said, "I mean, it's not like they can do anything. It happened outside school."

"Yes, but if those kids are being racist ..." she began.

"I'll be OK," I told her. "Go on. Stop worrying and get to work."

She came over and kissed me on the head.

"Be good," she told me.

"Always am," I said.

Ten minutes after she left, I went and got myself a drink. When I got back to the living room I saw that there was an argument on the talk show. I turned it up and watched.

There were two men sitting on either side of the presenter. One of them was white and the other Asian. The presenter was talking about

36

Christmas, just like we'd done at school.

"If they don't like it," the white man said, "then they should go on and get back to their own country."

Some of the people in the audience cheered and the rest of them booed. The Asian man looked really angry.

"But it is not our festival," he told the white man. "Why should we have this forced on us when we are not Christians?"

The presenter pointed out that Britain was a Christian country. That was just what Mr Abbas had said at school.

"But *we* are not Christians," the Asian guy said again.

Someone in the audience put up a hand and the camera cut to her. She was Asian and she had a headscarf like Samira, but it was black.

"I'm not sitting here," she said, "and listening to this rubbish. You can't cancel Christmas. We live in *this* country and we should take part in its festivals."

The audience went wild — the people were clapping and cheering so loudly.

"No one wants to cancel Christmas," said

the Asian guy. "We're just asking why we need to celebrate it when we are not Christians."

The woman in the audience shook her head.

"But white kids have to learn all about Eid and Diwali," she pointed out. "What's so different about Christmas?"

Again the audience clapped and cheered her and the Asian guy went red in the face. The white guy on the other side of the presenter stood up. He pointed at the Asian.

"Yeah!" he said, his face going red too. "And if you don't like it, get back to your own country ..."

The crowd booed him again, as the presenter ended the show with a cheesy smile. I changed the channel and sat back, thinking about how I was going to get Yusuf and his crew back.

Chapter 5
Making Friends

It was two weeks later and I'd made it to football practice at last. Nothing more had happened after the attack on me. Faz and the girls had made a fuss about it but I'd told them to forget it. It was just one of those things, I told them. I knew I was going to get Yusuf back — I was just waiting for the right time. And his crew had left me alone too, apart from calling me a few names. It was like, after they'd beat me up, they forgot about me. And that was fine with me.

It was really cold when I got outside. We were using the astro-turf pitches and Faz was waiting for me, along with Mr Lester.

"I'm looking forward to seeing you play," Mr Lester told me. "Faz said that you're very gifted."

I gave a shrug.

"I'm OK," I said. "Used to play loads."

Mr Lester smiled at me.

"We're a good side but we're short of a few

players. What position do you play?"

"Mid-field," I told him. "Or up front. I don't mind."

"Good, good," he said.

The practice was an hour and a half and when it was over, Mr Lester told me that I was definitely on the team.

"We've got a game on Saturday morning," he told me, "at a school out in the country."

I nodded.

"I'll be taking the mini-bus so you need to be at school for 9am. Is that OK?"

"Yeah," I said. "I'll be there."

On the way home, Faz came with me. I was OK, walking home alone, but he wanted to stick with me. I asked him about Yusuf and his crew.

"They're just bullies," he told me.

"Yeah, but they don't mess with you," I pointed out.

"They can't," he said with a smirk. "I'd batter 'em and they know it."

"They pick on my colour all the time," I told him.

"I know," Faz said. "They think it's clever but

they ain't got a clue."

I gave a shrug. "Maybe they've got a point?" I said. "I mean, I am in an Asian area."

Faz shook his head. "I don't go for that nonsense, blood," he said to me. "Them men is just stupid. Ain't no Asian areas and white areas. That's for racists..."

I nodded. "How come they don't like white people?" I asked.

"Same reason white racists don't like Pakis," he replied.

I was shocked that he'd used that word and he saw it on my face.

"'S'only a word," he added. "Racists are thick. Always blaming everyone else for their problems. Half my family are like Yusuf and them. Everything is the fault of white people, even though they create that crap for themselves, you get me?"

"My dad is like that," I said.

This time Faz looked shocked.

"Really?" he asked.

"Yeah. He's got all these tattoos and that. Hates anyone that ain't white."

Faz grinned. "He should hook up with Yusuf," he said. "They'd make a good team."

"My dad's mental," I said.

I told Faz all about why I'd ended up at my new school, and when I was done, he looked even more shocked than before.

"That's crazy, bro," he said. "No wonder you act odd."

I gave him a funny look. "How am I odd?" I asked.

"Trust me, bro," he said. "Like with Priya, you don't even notice the gal and she's well into you. And most of the time you don't say much."

"I guess so," I said softly.

I thought about Priya the rest of the way home. I'd only ever been out with one girl and even that was just for a week. Priya was cute too. The thought made me smile.

"You know it!" Faz said to me as we reached my block.

"Huh?" I asked.

"I know you're thinking about Priya," he told me. "Ask her out."

I shook my head. "I'd love to," I told him,

"but just think what Yusuf and them will do."

Faz grinned.

"Forget about them," he told me.

The next evening I met up with Faz by the shops and he took me round to his house.

When we got there his mum and dad were in the living room. They both smiled at me as his dad stood up. There were pictures on every wall, most of them of Mecca, and the room smelt really sweet.

"You must be David," said Faz's dad.

"Hello," I said.

"Welcome to our house. Faz's mum has made food and it'll be ready soon."

I said that I wasn't really very hungry but Faz's dad said I must eat something. In fact, I was hungry. I just didn't want to say. I was being polite.

"No one comes to this house and leaves without eating something," he told me. "That's the way we do things."

"OK," I said. "Thank you."

"No need to thank me, son," he said. "You are more than welcome."

"Come on, David, let's go and check out my room," said Faz.

As I left the living room an old woman came through from the kitchen. She looked at me and said something that I didn't understand. I smiled and said hello.

"That's my gran," Faz told me. "She lives with us."

"Hasn't she got a house of her own?" I asked.

Faz shook his head.

"Nah," he said. "This is her house too."

When he saw me look puzzled, he grinned.

"Don't worry," he told me, "It's an Asian thing, blood."

"Oh," I said, and I went up the stairs after him.

We spent an hour playing a zombie game on his X-Box before his dad gave us a shout. The food had been laid out on a table in the kitchen and the smell was amazing. I've always loved curry but whenever my mum gets some, it's always from the take-away. I'd never had curry at an Asian person's house before. It looked totally different.

"There's lamb and chicken," Faz's mum told me.

She was about as tall as my mum and really pretty. And her eyes were bright blue, the same as mine. I couldn't stop staring at them. I didn't know that Asian people could have blue eyes too.

"And try the samosas first," she went on. "I got them this afternoon."

I did what she said and took a samosa. Faz squirted some ketchup onto my plate and we sat down to eat. The food was delicious. I had chicken wings and lamb curry with rice after the samosa. By the time I was done, I was so full that I didn't want to move.

"The food was great," I told Faz's mum.

"Thank you, young man," she answered. "Come round any time you want some more. Bring your mum too."

I looked at Faz.

"They asked about you so I told them," he said.

"Everything?" I asked.

"No, not everything," he told me.

We went into the living room where his dad

was watching telly. I sat down on the sofa with Faz and looked at the TV screen.

"Faz tells me you've had some trouble at school," said his dad.

I nodded. "It's nothing," I told him. "Just some idiots, that's all."

"That's not what he told me," said Faz's dad.

I looked at Faz but he turned away.

"They picked on me because I'm white," I said at last.

"Well, you make sure that you stand up for yourself," his dad told me.

"I'll try," I said.

Faz's dad shook his head.

"There are too many people around who blame a person's colour for their own problems," he said. "You have to stand up to them."

"Things are OK now, Dad," said Faz. "They've forgotten about it."

That was what I thought too, but I was wrong. Things were about to get really ugly ...

Chapter 6
Matty and Priya

It started at the football game that Saturday. Some of the other lads in the team didn't want me to play. But Mr Lester had picked me and I was there. I stuck with Faz and another lad, Leon, who was black. The other team was made up of white lads and some of their supporters called us a few names when we came out of the changing rooms. Mr Lester told us to ignore them and just watch how we played. The game started well and I set up Leon for a goal. But a few minutes later, when I was about to take a throw in, someone called out my name. I threw the ball to Faz and then turned round. But there wasn't anyone I knew there so I ran onto the pitch.

Five minutes later I heard my name again. This time I thought that there must be some lad in the other team called David too. I turned back to the game. I needed to focus. Faz had the ball and he was bearing down on goal. I ran to get alongside him, shouting for him to put me through on goal. He waited until I made a run into the box and then slid the ball my way. It was the perfect pass. I wouldn't even have to control it. I made ready to hit the ball towards goal when I felt my leg go. Someone had tripped me up. I fell on my face.

"Traitor!" I heard someone say to me.

I turned round and saw a lad with a red face staring at me. The rest of my team wanted a penalty but the referee ignored them. He ran over to me.

"Get up, son!" he shouted. "He didn't touch you!"

I got up and told the ref I'd been tripped up but he just ran off again. I turned to the lad who'd fouled me.

"You want summat?" I asked him.

"Paki-lover!" he spat.

I wanted to smack him in the mouth but I didn't. I would have been sent off and that wouldn't help me or my team. Instead, I took up my position again.

Five minutes later I had the ball at my feet and I was not far from goal. I ran past two tackles and then let my shot go. The ball swerved in the air and flew into the net. My team mates went mad. They jumped on me and cheered. Once they'd stopped, I ran to the red-faced lad and taunted him.

"Pick that one out," I told him.

"You tosser!" he said. "Go back to Pakistan with your gay mates ..."

I laughed at him and went back to my position. The game kicked off and right away the ball went out of play. I ran to get it, ready to take another throw in. A big, bulky white man handed me the ball with a smile.

"Hello, David," he said.

I looked at him. He had a shaven head and piggy blue eyes. A tattoo ran from behind his left ear and down his neck.

"Remember me?" he added.

I shook my head, took the ball and threw it in. I *did* remember the man but I didn't want him to know. I felt sick and I started to sweat. The man who'd handed me the ball was my dad's best mate, Matty. He'd definitely tell my dad that he'd seen me and that would be that. It wouldn't take my dad long to find out where my school was. And then me and mum would have to move. Again! I just wanted the game to end. I didn't care about the result. I wanted to get home and warn my mum.

My mum put her head in her hands when I told her, later that afternoon.

"It'll be OK," I told her. "He won't find us."

But I didn't believe it. And neither did my mum.

"He always finds us," she said. "We should have just moved to a new city. It's my fault. I didn't want to go too far off."

I shook my head. "Why should we move?" I asked. "Sod him."

My mum gave a long sigh. "But he'll never leave us alone, David," she told me. "He'll turn up like a bad smell no matter where we are. He'll never stop ..."

I got up. I banged the work-top with my fist. "Yeah," I said, "but I'm a lot bigger than I was before. Let him come. I'll deal with him."

My mum shook her head.

"NO!" she shouted. "You're not to go near him, David. He's a psycho."

"If he comes here," I told her, "then I'm

gonna batter him."

"David ..." Mum began.

I didn't reply. Instead I went to my room and put on some music. I didn't want to move again. Even with all the problems with Yusuf and his crew and being the only white boy and all that. I liked my new mate, Faz and I wanted to ask Priya out. And I wanted to just chill and do my GCSEs. I wasn't going to pass them anyway but at least I had a chance if I stayed in one school for long enough. I wanted to get a good job and help my mum out. And I wanted to do loads of stuff, like go places and meet new people.

"He's not going to mess up my life again," I said out loud.

The problem was that he *was* going to mess it up. And mess it up good ...

I met Faz outside Lahore Fried Chicken later that night. He was standing with Priya and Sonia when I got there, eating from a box of hot wings. He gave me one and I took it.

"You OK?" Sonia asked me.

"Yeah," I said through a mouthful of chicken.

"Manners, young man!" laughed Priya.

I swallowed the chicken and looked at her. She was smiling at me. Her curly hair was tied up on her head and she was wearing a tight top and jeans with trainers. I couldn't stop looking at her eyes. They were light brown and they sparkled.

"I'm sorry," I said and I smiled back at her.

Faz grinned. "Stop saying you're sorry," he told me. "Girls like it when you order dem about, you get me?"

Sonia shook her head. "Is that why you ain't got a girl?" she asked him.

"I got loads of girls," he boasted. "I just ain't got time for them ..."

Priya told me that they were thinking of going to the cinema. I gave a shrug. I didn't have any money.

"I'm paying," said Faz. He saw I was embarrassed. "My dad gave me a wedge of money earlier. Anyway, David paid last time me and him went out."

I looked over to Faz but he turned away. I didn't know why he was lying but I was grateful. I didn't have any money at the best of times.

"My old man's got too much money

anyway," added Faz. "'Bout time he splashed out, the tight git."

"Cool!" said Sonia, taking Faz's hand. "You can buy me the biggest popcorn in the place."

"I think I've pulled," Faz said with a wink.

"What are we gonna watch?" I asked.

Priya grinned.

"Who cares?" she said. "You gonna hold my hand or what, white boy?"

I looked at Faz, who was smiling like a nutter.

"Go on, blood, what you waiting for?" he said.

Chapter 7
Flesh and Blood

The following Monday, at school, I wanted to talk to Faz. I wanted to tell him about seeing Matty, my dad's mate. But I never got the chance. Instead I spent break and lunchtime with Priya and at the end of school, I walked out with her. We weren't holding hands or anything but everyone could see that we were together. Faz was waiting for us outside the main doors. The three of us walked home together.

It was freezing cold and sleet was falling so Priya was all huddled up against me. Some of the Asian lads gave us dirty looks but I ignored them. Besides, Faz was with us and they were OK with him.

We'd only just left school when *he* turned up.

"Is this what it's come to?" he asked.

When I heard his voice, I felt sick. It was my dad. I turned to Faz and Priya and told them to go.

"Nah, blood," Faz told me.

"You heard him, Bin Laden," said my dad.

Faz turned to him and swore.

"Feisty little Paki, in't yer?" my dad went on.

"Just leave him alone," I said.

My dad smirked at me. "At least you're taking their bloody women," he said to me. "Good lad."

I told Priya and Faz to ignore my dad. I said I was sorry. "Just go," I said to them. "I'll call you both later."

"Yeah, run along," added my dad. "Mosque opens soon."

I watched them go and then I started walking away from my dad. Away from the shops and the flats.

"Hold on, son," said my dad. He had to run to catch me up.

He was even bigger than I remembered and he had a fresh tattoo on his neck. It was a bull-dog with a big Union Jack around it. His hair was shaved close to his scalp. He was wearing black boots, tight jeans and a black bomber jacket.

"How's things?" he asked me.

"None of your business," I said.

"It is my business though, in't it?" he said. "You're my son, my flesh and blood."

I shook my head.

"You ain't nothing to me," I told him. "I don't want you here and I don't want to talk to you. Just go away."

His face changed and he looked angry. I felt scared because I knew how violent he could be.

"What?" he shouted, as some of the other kids from school looked at us. "You'd rather hang around with Pakis?"

"Oh, just do one, you twat!" I said, but I was beginning to shake.

"They might as well give up round here," he added. He hadn't heard what I'd just said. "Why don't they just stick up a Paki flag and give the streets to them ..."

I started to walk again. Maybe then he'd just leave me alone. I noticed an old blue van pull up at the kerb. There was a St George's flag in the back window.

"I'll see you around," my dad said to me.

Then he got into the van and it sped off. Matty was driving it. I stopped and waited for it to go right away before I headed back to the shops. I knew my dad was gone but I still checked behind me every few minutes. Not that it mattered. He'd found me and now he wasn't going to leave me alone. I had to warn my mum.

But when I got in my mum had left me a note. She'd had to go into work early and was gone for the night. I thought about ringing her mobile. But then I decided not to. She'd only worry all night if I did. Instead I made myself something to eat and sat down in front of the telly. I had a load of homework to do but I couldn't focus on anything. All I could think about was my dad.

By eight o'clock I'd had enough and I decided to go for a walk. I rang Faz and we said we'd meet up outside Lahore Fried Chicken. It took me five minutes to get there — a bit before Faz. There were a few lads from school hanging around but no one who would give me too much grief. I had a few pound coins in my pocket so I went into the shop and got myself a chicken burger. I stood and ate it outside. It was still sleeting and there was a real chill in the air. I ate quickly before walking over to a bin to get rid of my rubbish. When I turned around I saw Yusuf, Tahir and the whole crew walking towards the shop. I stood still and watched them but I didn't back down. I didn't think that they would do anything but I was wrong.

"Your dad's a racist," Tahir said to me.

I gave a shrug. "So what?" I told him. "You are too."

"I seen him earlier," added Tahir. "He was talking about the mosque — bein' rude and disrespectful. You'd better tell him to watch his mouth. Ain't safe for a white man talking like that round here."

The rest of the crew backed Tahir up as I shook my head.

"He ain't nothing to do with me," I told them. "I don't even like the man."

Yusuf smirked at me.

"Typical white boy," he said. "Don't even stand up for his own kind. You ain't got no balls."

I got ready for a fight, but I was hoping that Faz was about to arrive.

"Faz is about to reach," I warned. "And then I know you lot are gonna run like girls."

"Faz?" spat Yusuf. "You think we're scared of that *bwoi*? He's whiter than you on the inside. Man's a traitor. And don't even deny that you're checkin' that slag Priya."

I wanted to knock him out but I held back. There were too many of them and I wasn't stupid. Suddenly I heard shouting.

"GET 'EM!" shouted someone.

I turned to see my dad, Matty and two other men running towards us.

"Here come your mates," said Yusuf, and he pulled out a blade.

A couple of their crew ran off but Tahir, Yusuf and the rest stood their ground.

"LEAVE HIM ALONE, YOU PAKI BASTARDS!" I heard my dad shout.

Yusuf pulled his hood over his head and got ready. Tahir had a steel baseball bat. He smacked me with it on the arm. The pain shot through me. I felt sick. I threw a punch but missed and then a riot started.

My dad and his mates jumped Yusuf and his crew and they all began to fight. I was busy trying to hold off Tahir. I stepped aside as he hit me with the bat again. This time I kicked him and the bat fell to the ground with a clink. I grabbed it and held it in front of me. Tahir jumped at me.

We ended up on the floor, rolling around, trying to batter each other. Suddenly I heard a shout and then someone screamed. I stopped fighting with Tahir. Both of us turned to see Yusuf lying on the ground. My dad was standing over him. He had Yusuf s blade in his hand.

"Ain't giving it now, are you?" spat my dad.

Tahir and all Yusuf's mates ran for it. Then I heard the police sirens. My dad turned to me.

"Come with us, son!" he shouted.

"NO!" I shouted back.

He looked at me for a moment, then Matty grabbed him.

"We need to go now!" Matty shouted. "Come on!"

As they ran off too, I knelt down beside Yusuf. His eyes were open but he was gasping for air. There was blood pouring from a hole in his chest. I put my hand hard over it to stop the bleeding and shouted for help. That was when I saw Faz.

"What happened?" he asked.

I shook my head.

"DAVID!" he yelled at me.

I looked up at him.

"My dad," I whispered.

Chapter 8
Doing the Right Thing

When the police let me go, my mum took me home. I'd been at the police station for about four hours. The police asked me the same questions over and over again. They wanted to know all about the fight and why I'd been attacked. When I told them that it was my dad that had stabbed Yusuf, they asked even more questions.

They tried to make out that I had called my dad to help me fight with Yusuf and his crew. But I didn't let them trick me. I pointed out that it was me who'd grassed up my dad. Why would I do that if he'd come to help me? Then my mum turned up and they stopped trying it on. My mum told them that she was going to ring a solicitor. She took a card out of her bag. "Someone at the hospital gave it to me," she said.

We were sitting in a waiting room. There were posters all over the wall for Crimestoppers and stuff like that. I sat back and closed my eyes. I hadn't told the police about my dad to start with. Not because I gave a toss about him. I didn't. But I didn't want to be a grass either. Then I started to think about Yusuf's mum and how she would be feeling. I knew how my mum would feel if it had been me that had been stabbed. That was what made me tell them.

"Why didn't you tell me he was back?" my mum asked me.

"I only saw him today," I told her. "I didn't think he'd turn up so quickly."

My mum sighed. "That's what he's like," she told me. "I'm sorry that I ever met him. I'm just glad to have you. At least something good came out of me and him."

I looked at her. "What if I turn out the same as him?" I asked. "It's possible, ain't it?"

She shook her head and pulled me to her. "You'll never be like him," she told me. "You've shown me that today. You did the right thing telling the police about him. That man is an animal."

She kissed me on the head.

"And I think you probably helped save that

lad's life when you held your hand over where he'd been stabbed," she added. "That was really smart of you."

"Did the police tell you anything about how Yusuf is?" I asked.

"No, love," my mum told me. "I'll call the hospital when we get home."

And when we got in, that's what she did. I made us both cups of tea and we went and sat in the living room. She looked grim as she listened to one of her work mates tell her what was going on. Then she put the phone down and turned to me.

"He'll be OK," she told me. "But he's very badly hurt."

I nodded.

"And was he one of the boys who was bullying you?" she asked.

"Yeah," I said.

"See?" she pointed out. "What you did today, to help that lad, just shows you're not like your dad. You could have just run away."

I thought about telling her how I'd planned to get Yusuf back for beating me up. Did that make me a good person too? But in the end I was too tired and I just wanted to get into bed.

I didn't even drink my tea. I said goodnight and went to my room.

In the morning my mum told me it was OK for me to stay off school. She rang and spoke to Mr Abbas. He asked her if he could come round and my mum said that'd be fine but she wouldn't be there. She had to go to work.

"Will you be OK?" she asked me as she left.

"Yeah, Mum, I'll be fine. Can you leave me some money for food?"

She gave me a fiver and told me to be good. Then she grabbed her stuff and left. I made some toast and ate a bit. Then I just sat in front of the telly, not really watching it. All I could think about was my dad. I wondered whether the police had caught him and what he'd be thinking. He'd know that I'd grassed him up and I knew he'd be angry. What if he got away and tried to attack me or mum? The thought went round and round in my head. In the end I was so worried I went back to bed. But I couldn't sleep.

At lunchtime the buzzer went. I walked to the intercom and asked who was there. It was Mr Abbas and Faz. I buzzed them in and went to open the door. We sat in the living room and Mr Abbas asked me how I was feeling.

"I'm fine," I told him. "I just want to chill for a bit."

"I understand," he told me. "It must have been really difficult for you. Not just the fight, but then telling the police about your dad."

I shook my head.

"I don't like my dad," I told him. "That wasn't difficult. He's a psycho and it's better if he's in jail. Especially for me and my mum."

"Everyone was talking about it at school," Faz told me.

"Did Priya say anything?" I asked.

"Yeah, she wanted to come round. But she had to work on some project for the library," he said.

"Can you tell her I'll call her later? I haven't got any credit on my phone."

Faz grinned. "As always," he joked.

Mr Abbas asked me why the fight had started.

"It was Yusuf," I told him. "Him and his mates jumped me when I was waiting to meet

Faz. And then my dad and his mates turned up and they all started fighting."

"And your dad had a knife?" he asked.

I shook my head.

"Nah, it was Yusuf's blade an' that. He pulled it first. My dad must have got it off him when they were fighting ..."

Mr Abbas shook his head. "I don't know what's wrong with these people," he said.

"What people?" Faz asked him.

"All these racists," Mr Abbas said. "I mean, where's it got Yusuf or David's dad? How does it help anyone to hate people who are different from them?"

I gave a shrug.

"My dad deserves to go to prison again," I said.

"And what about Yusuf?" asked Mr Abbas.

"He shouldn't have been stabbed," I said. "But he was trying to do me. If my dad hadn't come along, he'd have used that knife on me ..."

"Exactly," replied Mr Abbas. "Why did he have the knife in the first place?"

Faz butted in. "It was on the local news this

morning. They said that it was a racist attack by a bunch of white men."

I shook my head. "Well, that's just stupid then, innit?" I said. I felt angry. "How come it's always just white people who get the blame for racist attacks?"

Faz and Mr Abbas looked at me.

"Yusuf and his crew are just as racist as my dad," I told them. "But no one's going to know about that. It's just gonna be another white man that did it ..."

Faz gave a shrug. "I didn't think about that," he admitted. "You're right, too."

I looked at Mr Abbas.

"Did you tell the police that Yusuf was racist to you?" he asked me.

I nodded.

"No one cares about that," I said. "It don't make the news. Like I said, I don't even *like* my dad. But he weren't the only racist in that fight, was he?"

"How long will he go away for?" asked Faz.

I gave a shrug.

"Don't know, don't care," I told him. "The

police have got him locked up."

"But you'll have to go to court," Mr Abbas pointed out. "You'll have to be a witness against your dad."

I nodded. "If that's what it takes," I said.

We talked about it for a bit longer and then Mr Abbas said that him and Faz had to get back to school.

"We'll see you tomorrow," he said to me.

"Yeah," I said. "I'll be there."

"If you need to talk to anyone," he added, "just let me know."

I smiled. "Thanks, sir," I said.

"At least it's all over now," he said. "Things should be a lot easier from now on."

I saw them out and then went back into the living room. My dad would be going away again, so things would be a lot less difficult for me and my mum. We wouldn't have to move. Maybe I could stay at my new school until the end of Year 11. I relaxed as I thought about seeing Priya the next day, and then I fell asleep.

Chapter 9

Them and Us

It was on Christmas Eve that I knew my troubles weren't over. I was at the bus stop with Priya. She was standing in front of me and I had my hands under her jacket to keep them warm. We'd just been to see a film and were on our way back home. My mum had asked Priya to come over and eat with us and she was coming over that day.

I was really happy. School had got much better and everyone seemed to like me. I had lots of new mates and I had Priya. I was even settling into lessons and starting to learn stuff.

I hadn't been able to do that for ages. And no one called me white boy any more, not in a racist way.

It was because I was happy that I didn't see him coming. If I'd have been watching for trouble, I'd have been looking around. But I wasn't feeling paranoid any more. I'd helped to save Yusuf s life and grassed up his killer. What did I have to worry about?

He was right behind me before I saw him. I turned round and there was Tahir. He was all twisted up with hate.

"This ain't over, white *bwoi*," he spat. "Not ever."

Priya answered for me.

"Are you mental?" she asked Tahir. "David saved Yusuf's life!"

Tahir didn't even look at her.

"You gonna get yours," he said to me. "One of these days when you ain't thinkin' about it ..."

"If that's how you want it," I said, and I turned away.

Tahir smirked. "White bastard!" he spat and then walked off.

I watched him go as Priya took my hand.

"Don't worry about him," she said.

I told her that I wasn't worried. But it was a lie. I was going to have to keep on watching my back all the time. I suppose I'd got used to it. I was just going to have to deal with more trouble when it came. I pulled Priya close to me and gave her a kiss.

"Come on," I said as I smiled at her. "The bus is takin' ages. Let's walk back."

Author's Note

I wrote *Them and Us* as a companion piece to my earlier book, *What's Your Problem?* The latter was a more traditional take on racial prejudice, with a non-white victim. *Them and Us*, however, was conceived as a mirror image, with a white, British teenager as the central figure. I'd always intended the two to be read together, so I'm delighted to see *Them & Us* back in print.

Two aspects of racism inspired the book. The first is that racial prejudice exists in the UK, and despite claims to the contrary, is still a major problem. From the surge in Islamophobia to anti-foreigner, anti-immigrant rhetoric, recently disguised as patriotism around the Brexit debacle, and the suspicious deaths of black Britons in police custody, racial intolerance weaves an ugly seam through the heart of British society.

The second was my own experience of racist attitudes within my family. From early childhood, I heard various family members make prejudiced remarks about other races, religions and cultures. From the talk of "dirty white people" to "robbing, drug-dealing blacks", the attitudes amongst some of my relatives were no different to those of the racist white Britons they complained about. In fact, breaking free of this familial prejudice was the main drive for my rebellious teenage years. I can't even begin to recall how many arguments and debates (and actual fights) I was involved in as a result.

So, after *What's Your Problem?* was published, I felt like a hypocrite. How could I write about the racial prejudice of white Britons and ignore that of people who looked like me? And then, during a school visit, I met a young white British teen called David, one of only a handful of white pupils in a school population of fifteen hundred, in an area renowned locally as being "Asian". This young man was bullied for being different, bullied for being part of a minority, bullied, yes, for being white.

And that's the crux of it, for me. It is simple and easy to write about the racial prejudice of white Britons. The same is not true in reverse. Because of misguided ideas about cultural sensitivity, many politicians and commentators shirk away from confronting the prejudice that exists amongst Britain's Black and Minority Ethnic communities.

And racial prejudice has never been as simple as "whites are racist" and the rest aren't. It's far more complex, far more nuanced than that. Especially in twenty-first century Britain, where population and social changes have created inner-city areas in which the wider majority-white population have become the minority.

Them and Us is an attempt to explore some of the issues already mentioned, as openly and honestly as possible. There are no quick fixes, no easy solutions – it is, at heart, just a story. But stories can help bridge divides amongst people, and I hope that this book can play some small part in doing just that.

Bali Rai